Cold Little Duck, Duck, Duck

by **Lisa Westberg Peters**

Pictures by **Sam Williams**

Greenwillow Books • *An Imprint of HarperCollinsPublishers*

Pencil and watercolors were used for the full-color art.
The text type is Bauer Bodoni Black BT.

Cold Little Duck, Duck, Duck

Text copyright © 2000 by Lisa Westberg Peters Illustrations copyright © 2000 by Sam Williams.
Printed in Hong Kong by South China Printing Company (1988) Ltd. All rights reserved.
http://www.harperchildrens.com

Library of Congress Cataloging-in-Publication Data

Peters, Lisa Westberg.
Cold little duck, duck, duck / by Lisa Westberg Peters ; pictures by Sam Williams.
p.   cm.   "Greenwillow Books."
Summary: Early one spring a little duck arrives at her pond and finds it still frozen, but not for long.
ISBN 0-688-16178-2 (trade).   ISBN 0-688-16179-0 (lib. bdg.)
[1. Ducks—Fiction.   2. Spring—Fiction.   3. Stories in rhyme.]
I. Williams, Sam, ill.   II. Title.   PZ8.3.P443Co 2000   [E]—dc21   99-29880   CIP

1 2 3 4 5 6 7 8 9 10 First Edition

For Becky
—L. W. P.

For Linda—my spring in winter
—S. W.

One miserable and frozen spring

brisk

brisk brisk

A cold little duck flew in

BRR-ACK BRR-ACK BRR-ACK

Her pond was stiff and white

creak creak creak

And her feet froze to the ice

stuck

stuck

stuck

stuck

You're way too early, Duck, go back

back

back

You're beginning to shiver, Duck

shake shake

shake shake

She tucked her head into her feathers to think

think think

Of spring and warmer weather

warmer weather

quick   *quick*   *quick*

Of bubbly
streams
and
glassy
puddles

DRINK
DRINK

DRINK

Of
wiggly worms
and shiny
beetles

black

black

black

Of crocuses
and apple
buds

pink
pink *pink*

And blades of grass in squishy mud

snack
snack
snack

Her thoughts
of spring
filled the sky

thick

thick

thick

Until a V of ducks flew by

flock

flock

flock

They saw that spring was in the air

blink blink blink

And quickly spreading everywhere

look

look

look

The ducks flew down, they dipped and splashed

dunk

dunk

dunk

Come join us, Duck, it's melting fast

shrink

shrink

shrink

The cold little duck began to slide

slick slick slick

Across the disappearing ice

CRACK

CRACK

CRRR . . . . ACK

She wiggled her tail, waggled her wings

kick

kick

kick

The warm little duck dove into spring

Quack

Quack